THE ADVENTURES OF MICKI MICROBE

by
Maurine Burnham Guymon

illustrated by
Arlene Tucker Zagone

*This book is dedicated to
my students who were
enlightened and
enchanted by the
adventures of
microbes.*

*This book designed by
Arlene Tucker Zagone*

*Printed by Publishers Press
and bound by
Mountain States Bindery
Salt Lake City, Utah*

MoDel Publishers, P.O. Box 645, Byron, California 94514-0645

PREFACE

During my many years of teaching, one message came through to me: "If you have a winner, keep it running".

As I look back on my twenty years of teaching in the elementary grades I remember some of our most enjoyable and relaxing times as a class were the fifteen or twenty minutes of oral reading sandwiched into a busy schedule—a rest after lunch, a few extra minutes before going home—a book was always ready on the corner desk. Of course, the classic children's books were always available and will never be forgotten, but there was another book that made a big impact on my 2nd, 3rd and 4th grade students and I do not like to see it lost on the generation of my grandchildren.

In my early years of teaching my mother handed me two old well worn books titled THE ADVENTURES OF JIMMY MICROBE and HITCH HIKING WITH JIMMY MICROBE, written by Virginia Jacobsen and Lyman Luther Daines, M.D., copyright 1937, illustrated by Kay Russon.

The first time I introduced the book to a 3rd grade class and realized the interest and enthusiasm generated by the students, I became a "Jimmy Microbe" fan. My mother, also a teacher, and I would trade the book back and forth during the school year because it was out of print and we could not purchase another copy. As I read the book I had to ad-lib or re-write sections to update the story.

During parent conferences many parents commented on the interest generated by Jimmy's adventures. During the years as I have met my former students, several have referred to our reading of the microbe book and the activities it generated such as growing bacteria and yeasts, writing their own microbe adventures, and of course, the great art work. Indeed, it made a lasting impression.

Now, as I have retired from teaching and think back on my career, I do not like to think of Jimmy Microbe lost to future generations. I have taken the books, and re-written them under the title of THE ADVENTURES OF MICKI MICROBE. I have modernized the story and made it more meaningful to present times. I'm sure the lessons contained will make an unforgettable impression on youthful readers.

I was fortunate in making the aquaintance of the talented artist, Arlene Zagone. Her illustrations capture the imagination of both young and old.

CONTENTS

Multiplication of Micki

Micki was really a good little microbe, but he was inquisitive and adventurous, and sometimes he roamed into odd places, met bad microbes and had frightening experiences. Micki belonged to a fine family called the Lactic Acid Family, but his curiosity often led him into mischief and trouble.

Our introduction to Micki finds him sitting on a rainbow bubble of milk wishing he could see more than the white liquid around him. He had no way of moving himself but he was anxious to discover a means of getting around and finding out what was happening in other places.

The glass of milk was sitting on the corner of the table and the rays of the afternoon sun were dancing on the surface. All of a sudden, while Micki was enjoying the warm sunshine, an amazing thing happened. Micki began to swell up like a balloon. He grew bigger and bigger. Then, strange to say, he began to grow smaller and smaller right in the middle, just as if some-one had tied a string around the center of him and was pulling it tighter and tighter. He was sure he would be cut in two.

Micki wiggled and squirmed, but the more he wiggled and the more he squirmed the smaller and smaller his waist grew.

"Oh!" wailed Micki. "What is going to happen to me?"

Just as he cried out, he swelled up still bigger. Then POP! Something had happened. Exactly as Micki Microbe had feared, he was cut into two pieces. While he was trying to figure out what was happening, Maggie came into the kitchen, reached over the edge of the table, picked up the glass and swallowed some of the milk.

As Micki found himself entering a large cave he heard Maggie call, "Mom, this milk tastes yukky!"

"Who left it out of the refrigerator?" asked Mother. "You had better pour the rest into the sink."

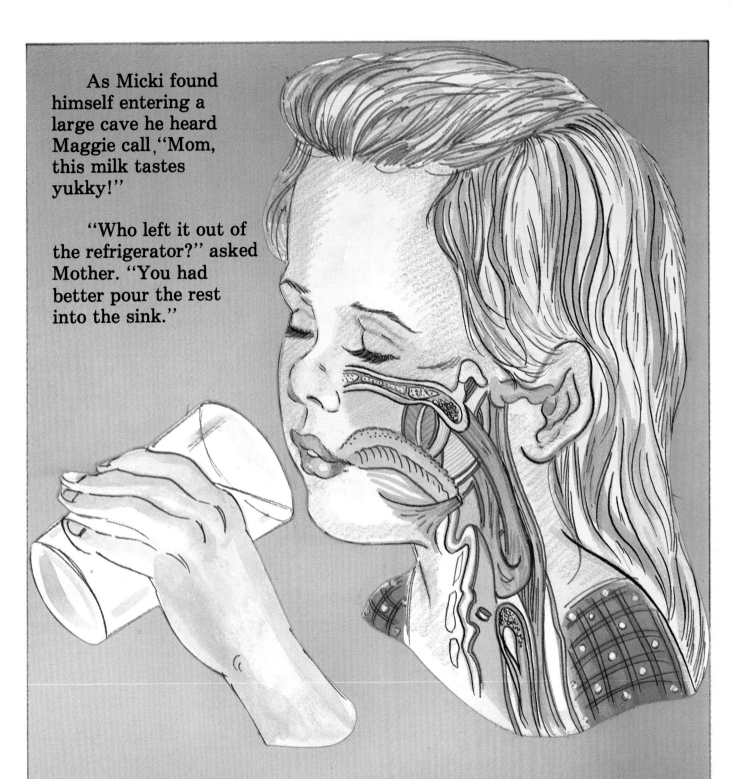

This was just the chance Micki Microbe was hoping for. Here he was taking a ride in a drop of milk, off to exciting places and new adventures. He was a little dizzy from his topsy turvy ride and settled down on a soft pink spot to try and catch his breath. This was the most peculiar place he had ever seen. There were big white cliffs and small red rolling hills; but it was warm and soft so he was happy to look around and take a short rest on the soft cushion.

While Micki was looking around at his new resting spot, he heard a laughing sound and next to him he saw a jolly little microbe swelling up into a big balloon; then growing tiny in the center and popping into two microbes.

"What are you doing?" asked Micki, remembering his own experience and hoping this new acquaintance could tell him what had happened.

"I am dividing and multiplying," answered the jolly microbe. Micki didn't know much about arithmetic and he certainly couldn't understand how you could divide to multiply, but the little microbes were now having such a great time he decided he would like to stay with them and join in the fun.

"Where are we?" asked Micki.

"We are in Maggie's Throat Street. It is a good place to divide and multiply, it is so warm and dark and moist," one microbe answered; and they continued their merry way of swelling up and dividing.

Micki joined in the laughing and fun making and decided he was going to enjoy his new friends and learn a lot from them.

"Who are you?" asked Micki.

"We are Pneumococci," answered two of his new friends that were staying close together. "Who are you?"

"I am Micki Microbe, one of the Lactic Acid Family," answered Micki. There was much to be proud of in belonging to the Lactic Acid Family.

"You sound very important. Where do you live and what do you do?" asked one of the Pneumococcus.

"I live in Milky Land. We Lactic Acid Microbes help to turn milk and cream into butter and cheese. We are proud of the fact that we are kind and helpful to man; but I'm tired of working all the time. I would like to wander around and find out what other things are happening."

"Well, you certainly came to the right place for adventures. Come with me and my twin and we'll show you the strangest sights you have ever seen. Just call us Pneumo 1 and Pneumo 2."

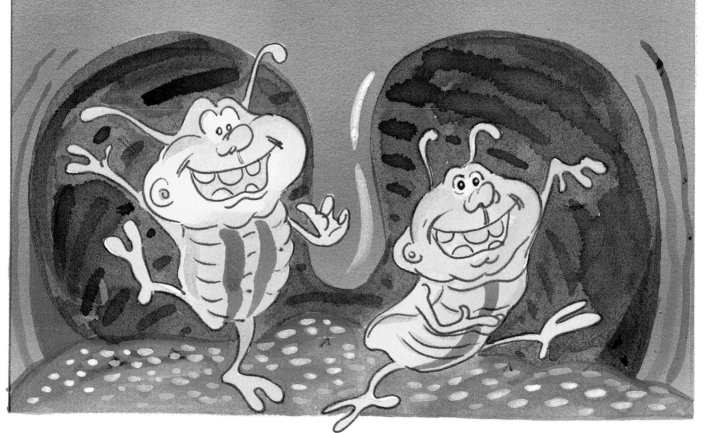

Throat Street

"Where do you live?" Micki asked his new acquaintances. "We live in a big double house which has hundreds of rooms. Our home is called Lung House. If you follow Throat Street over the top of Tongue Hill, you come to Windpipe Lane which leads you right to our house," explained Pneumo 1.

"That sounds exciting! I'd like to go there with you sometime," said Micki. "What is that pink cushiony place over there?"

"That is Tonsil Park, a playground for all kinds of microbes," answered Pneumo 2. "There is another one just like it on the other side of Throat Street. There are great places in Tonsil Park to hide, and there you can divide and multiply as fast as you want."

"What are those big white hills up there?" Micki asked.

"They are the White Teeth Hills and the Molar Mountains," replied the Pneumo Twins. "Some of them have big caves and cavities where we go exploring. The caves make good places in which to divide and mutiply."

"Hey! Let's go exploring now," said the excited Micki.

"O.K. Let's go to our house first," said Pneumo 1.

Micki Microbe was delighted because he wanted to see the big house where the Pneumo Twins lived.

Micki Microbe and the Pneumos started up Throat Street. It was slippery going over the top of Tongue Hill and very steep as they skidded down the hill.

"Follow me!" Called Pneumo 1. "We turn down Windpipe Lane in a minute."

As they turned down Windpipe Lane, a real obstacle confronted them. All down the lane there were little things like very tiny hairs which pointed up toward Throat Street. They were so tiny you could not see them unless you looked through a microscope. They seemed to be gently moving to and fro all the time. Micki was surprised at the difficulty he had trying to get through them.

"What is this forest of little hairs all down Windpipe Lane?" Micki asked the Pneumos.

"This is the Hairy Forest. It is here to protect our house. Lung House must be kept very clean and these tiny hairs act as a strainer to keep out particles of food, dust and microbes," explained the Pneumococci.

"Can we get through them?" asked the worried Micki.

"It may take a long time, but we can get through them if we try hard and long enough. But the Hairy Forest is not the greatest danger we have to pass," Pneumo 2 continued in a chilling whisper. "We have to sneak by Old Cough, the watch dog!"

"Is he very mean?" Micki was beginning to be a little frightened.

"No, he isn't mean, but he can have a terribly loud bark. Most people get very concerned when he begins to make a noise. If we go very slowly and quietly, he may not hear us," whispered Pneumo 1.

So Micki Microbe and the Pneumococci started to make their way very quietly through the tiny hairs which kept waving back and forth so rapidly that it was very hard to get through them.

"Say Pneumo," whispered the worried Micki, "if it is so difficult to get down to your house, how can we ever get up the hill to get out?"

"Getting out is not so hard. You see, the hairs point up the hill and make a stairway to climb on," explained Pneumo 1.

All of a sudden, Old Cough, the watch dog, discovered the tiny microbes trying to get down the hill to Lung House. It was his job to keep them away. He started barking and barking, trying to drive them out. He knew the twin Pneumos were bad little microbes and he supposed that Micki must be bad, too, or he would not be trying to visit Lung House with them. But Micki was not bad, he just did not know what kind of microbes the Pneumos really were or he would not have played with them.

Micki and the Pneumos crouched low. They were waiting for Old Cough to stop barking so that they could continue their journey down to Lung House.

Cough the Watch Dog

Windpipe Lane was very drafty. Each warm breeze blowing up and down the lane threatened to shake the little microbes loose.

"Hold on, or Old Cough will surely drive you out," whispered Pneumo 1. Old Cough finally quit barking but the tiny microbes were quietly waiting for a while before attempting to travel on. The Pneumos knew exactly what to do, for they had been through this experience many times before.

"What made Old Cough bark so loudly?" asked Micki.

"We did," replied the Pneumos in unison. "Everytime anyone starts down Windpipe Lane, Old Cough tries to drive him out."

Micki was so interested in what the Pneumos were telling him, that he forgot to hold on tightly. The next minute Old Cough started to bark again. Micki Microbe was so startled that he let go. He went whirling out of Windpipe Lane up into Throat Street and there he was picked up by a tiny drop of moisture. He went flying up Throat Street, past Tonsil Park, past the White Teeth Hills and out into the air.

After sailing around for a moment in the drop of moisture, Micki landed on a rubber ball which Maggie was holding. Everything seemed to be spinning around, Micki was so dizzy from his whirling ride. Gradually he began to look around and tried to realize what had happened. He could not see his Pneumococci friends, but there were hundreds of other little microbes on the ball all around Micki.

"The PneumoTwins must
have held on when I let go
down there in Windpipe Lane,"
thought Micki. "I wonder if I
will ever see them again." Micki
had no idea what a strange experience he would have in
Lung House with the Pneumos
on another day.

Just then Micki, and all the other little microbes on the ball, were startled when Maggie threw the ball down on the floor and it bounced toward a corner of the room. Maggie's little brother, Jamie, took a popsicle stick out of his mouth, threw it in the sink, and ran to get the ball.

"That's my ball!" Jamie yelled, as he caught the ball with his sticky fingers. He put his thumb right on the spot where Micki and all the other little microbes lay.

Of course, the microbes were so small that Jamie could not feel them there, but they were there just the same. In a minute he put his thumb in his mouth to try and lick off the sticky popsicle and he left Micki and some other little microbes floating around in his saliva.

Micki found himself back in Throat Street again. He wondered if there were any Tonsil Parks along this street. He decided to find out, so he slid along Tongue Road. Sure enough, there were two little Tonsil Parks, one on each side of the hill. There he came upon an amazing sight.

The Roly Poly Microbe

When Micki Microbe arrived in Jamie's Tonsil Park, he saw the strangest little microbes he had ever seen. They were round and small and joined together in chains like strings of beads. Some of the chains were made of four microbes, others of six and eight. Some were so long that Micki could not count them.

As Micki stood there watching them, one of the microbes called out to the others, "Hi, fellows, let's see who can divide and multiply the fastest."

Then all of the chains of microbes stopped playing and began to swell up like tiny balloons. Just as Micki had divided in two, each ball-shaped microbe divided right in the middle. This made just twice as many microbes in each chain as there had been a moment before. Where there had been four, there were now eight, and where there had been six, there were now twelve. To Micki's suprise, some of the long chains broke into two or three smaller chains. The dividing and multiplying and breaking up of the long chains went on and on as if the race would never end.

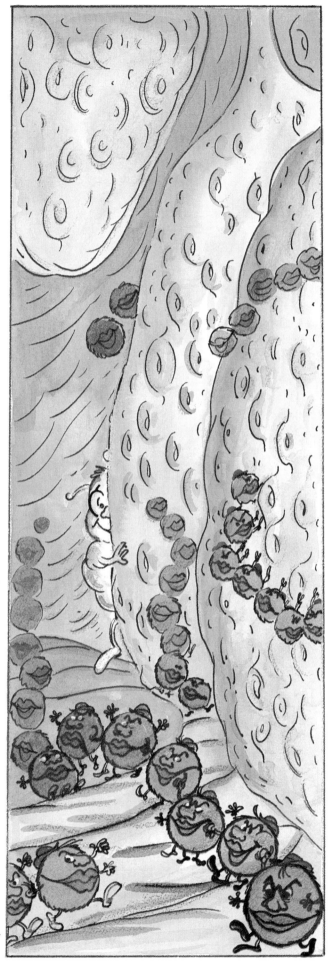

Micki noticed a roly-poly microbe standing not far away. He was watching the chains of microbes, too.

"Hi," said Micki to the roly-poly microbe.

"Oh, hello," replied the stranger. "They are funny aren't they?" he asked, pointing to the chains of bead-like microbes.

"Who are they?" asked Micki.

"They are members of the Streptococcus family, and are wicked. They think it would be great fun to make Jamie very sick," explained the roly-poly microbe.

Micki was horrified, "Will they hurt us?"

"No, they can't hurt us, but they will probably make Jamie sick and spoil Throat Street so that we can't stay here. Mt. T, a scout, will call out all his policemen to fight the Streptococcus Microbes and then if Jamie gets very sick his mother will call the doctor and get some medicine that will help kill the bad microbes. There will really be a war here and it will not be safe for us to stay."

"Then let's go now before anything like that happens!" Micki did not like the thought of being around when the medicine started to kill the chains of microbes. He certainly wasn't interested in staying around and making friends with these wicked germs.

"Oh, we have plenty of time. Those microbes will keep on dividing and multiplying until there are many more of them before they make Jamie sick. We have time to take a short nap," replied the roly-poly microbe.

"Who are you?" asked Micki.

"I am Staphylococcus. Just call me Staph," answered the roly-poly one in a friendly manner.

"Are you a friend of those terrible Streptococcus Microbes?" Micki asked in a trembling voice. Perhaps he would not like this new acquaintance after all.

"We are distantly related, but I'm not proud of the fact that we are related at all, and I don't see them very often."

"Where do you live?" asked Micki, who wanted to know everything about everyone.

"I live in the skin in a very small house called Pimple Cottage. One of my cousins lives in a house much larger than ours, called Boil Bungalow," replied Staphylococcus.

"If you live in the skin, how did you happen to be in Throat Street?" inquired Micki.

"Well, I really wanted to build a cottage on Jamie's chin," explained Staph. "There was a tiny scratch in his skin and I thought it might be a fine place for a Pimple Cottage; but it started itching and Jamie scratched the exact spot where I was sitting. I was caught on the edge of his finger nail and when he licked his sticky finger I found myself here in Throat Street."

By this time Micki and Staph were growing sleepy. They cuddled down in a warm spot in Tonsil Park and were soon fast asleep, forgetting all about the dreadful Streptococcus Microbes who were dividing and mulytiplying as fast as they could.

An Unexpected Journey

Micki Microbe awoke from his nap with a terrible start. Someone was poking him.

"Hey Micki! Wake up! We must get out of here." It was Staph calling and he seemed very excited.

"What's the matter?" asked Micki, still half asleep. "Why is it so hot in here?"

"Those dreadful Streptococcus Microbes are making Jamie sick. It is getting too hot in here to be comfortable," replied Staph.

"Do the Streptococci make it hot like this?" asked Micki.

"No. That is the way the body tries to get rid of the bad microbes who make children sick. A guard, Mr. T, calls out all the policemen to fight the germs and the body makes it hot so that we can't divide and multiply," answered the knowledgeable Staph.

There was great excitement in Jamie's Throat Street and Tonsil Parks. Micki could see hundreds of little microbes racing around. It was all very confusing to Micki.

"Come on, Staph. Let's get out of here," coaxed Micki.

Just then Jamie started to cry. "My throat hurts, I can't swallow!"

Mother came over and felt Jamie's hands and forehead. "Jamie, I believe you have a fever. Maggie, please bring me a thermometer and a spoon, I want to look at Jamie's throat. She put the spoon in Jamie's mouth to hold down his tongue. Then she looked at the red throat where all the little microbes were playing. She could not see them there because they were very small, but she knew that there must be microbes there or Jamie's throat would not be so red.

"Jamie, I want you to get in bed and try and get some sleep," said Mother. "I'll call the doctor and see if I can get some medicine for you."

"It is too late to get away," thought Micki.

When Mother took Jamie into the bedroom, little Allie Ann was playing on the bedroom floor. She stood up to look at Jamie and see why he was crying. Just then Jamie sneezed. Micki and hundreds of the little microbes went whirling out of Throat Street in tiny droplets of water. Most of them landed on Allie Ann's face and hands because she was standing right in front of Jamie.

Micki was quite surprised to find that Staphylococcus and some of the Streptococcus family were lying there close beside him on Allie Ann's face. They were near one of the openings to Nose Cave. It looked dark and mysterious. One of the little microbes called, "Follow me! I'll show you some fun."

Micki knew that he should not stay here with the bad microbes, but the thought of exploring this dark cave was so exciting he decided to go anyway.

Micki Explores Nose Cave

The entrance to Nose Cave was partially covered with a growth of little hairs which made it difficult to enter.

"What are all those hairs for?" asked one of the microbes.

"They must be for protection," proudly explained Micki. "Windpipe Lane is lined with tiny hairs, much smaller than these. The Pneumococcus Twins told me they worked as a strainer to keep the dirt out of Lung House. These must be for the same purpose, to keep Nose Cave clean."

"Well, they certainly do make it hard to get into the cave," replied Streptococcus. He was having a difficult time getting the long chain of microbes through the hairy growth.

It was dark inside, but the microbes were not afraid, they were too interested in trying to find out what was at the other end of the cave. As they slowly climbed up the hairy ladder, a little stream of water came trickling down and carried away several of the microbes.

Near the top of the cave, Micki and his companions came upon the tiniest microbes they had ever seen. They were so small that Micki could hardly see them in the darkness. They were far too small to be seen even through the microscope, but Micki could see them. He wondered who these wee microbes could be and what they were all doing in Nose Cave.

"They must be the Cold-In-The-Head Microbes," whispered one of Micki's companions. "They made that river flow down the cave. See! There, they sent another stream flowing down."

All of a sudden, the microbes found themselves at the top of the hill in Nose Cave. It was steeper than ever on this side of the hill. "Let's race and see who can get to the bottom of the hill first," yelled one of the microbes. They were all tired from climbing up the hill and the idea of going down a steep slide seemed like a great idea.

"Hooray!" they shouted, and down they went.

Imagine their suprise when they found themselves lying in Throat Street.

"Well! Who would ever guess this?" exclaimed Micki. Nose Cave opens right into Throat Street!"

"Whoopy!" squealed the Streptococcus Microbes. "Look at the big Tonsil Parks. We just love this place to play. Watch us divide and multiply! Won't we have fun!" Then they started to swell up and divide. They did not waste a minute.

Just then Mother must have noticed the little rivers flowing out of Allie Ann's Nose Caves. Micki heard her say, "Allie Ann you must have a cold, too. Let me look at your throat and see if it is red like Jamie's."

Mother picked up a spoon and pressed the handle down on Allie Ann's tongue so she could see down Throat Street. Micki thought he was lucky because the spoon touched the exact spot where he and some of the other microbes lay.

"Cling tightly to the spoon," whispered Micki. "This might be our only chance to escape before Mother gives Allie Ann some medicine and starts trouble for all of us. Some of the microbes held onto the spoon with Micki, but other Streptococci felt right at home in Throat Street and were happy to stay there and take their chances.

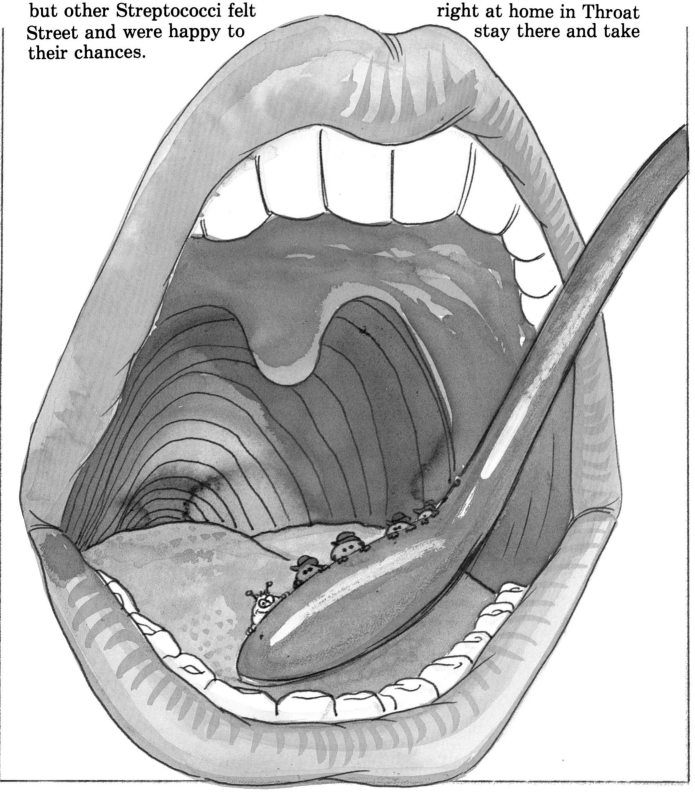

Mother carried the spoon out to the kitchen and left it on the sink. Micki stayed there on the spoon for quite sometime. There was no moisture to swim in and as he looked at the strange microbes around him he began to think of his own home and wonder if he would ever see any of his family again.

Just as he was beginning to feel a little homesick, Maggie came running into the kitchen.

"Mom, I'm going to make me some chocolate milk," she called. She took a carton out of the refrigerator and poured some milk into a glass. Now, it just happened, that instead of taking a clean spoon out of the drawer, she picked the one up from the sink — the exact one Micki was on. Micki first found himself covered with chocolate powder and the next thing he knew he was swimming around in his own home.

Home Again

Micki Microbe was so excited about being home again he did not realize the danger of ending up in Maggie's Throat Street. While Maggie was stirring her chocolate milk, her friend, Jennifer, called and said "Come outside and see my new bicycle!"

Micki floated around trying to find some of his family. He discovered some of the bad microbes had been washed off the spoon into the milk with him. He didn't like to see them in his nice clean home. Just then several members of Micki's family floated over to him and wanted to know where he had been. He told them about his strange adventures in Throat Street, Tonsil Park, Windpipe Lane, and Nose Cave. He told them about the Pneumo Twins, Staph, Streptococcus, and Cold-in-the-Head.

"Well," said one of his Lactic Acid Brothers, "so you brought those bad microbes home with you. That is the kind of friends you have been playing with!"

"Oh, no!" denied Micki. "They are not really my friends. They just happened to be in the same places I was. I wasn't really playing with them."

"Well, don't you know that if you are seen with bad microbes, folks will think you are bad, too?" said one of the Lactic Acid Brothers. He swam over close to Staphylococcus and asked in an angry voice, "Who are you and what are you doing here, I'd like to know?"

Staph was very suprised at someone so much like Micki being so cross. "I was caught on the spoon in Throat Street and then stirred into the milk with the chocolate," he explained in a timid voice.

Micki felt a little sorry for Staphylococcus being scolded in such a cross manner. "You see, Staph, this milk is our home. We live in the milk so that we can help make it into butter and cheese. If it were not for the Lactic Acid Family, people could not have good butter and cheese to eat. We don't spoil the milk because we are supposed to live here."

Several of the microbes had come closer to hear what Micki was saying. Micki continued in a louder voice, "After the milk was milked from the cow, it was pasteurized to kill any bad microbes which happened to be in the milk."

"What does pasteurized mean?" asked one of the microbes.

"It means that the milk was heated to just the right temperature to kill all the bad microbes," explained Micki proudly. "They call it that because a man named Pasteur was the first person to do it. After the milk was pasteurized, it was put into cartons or bottles and closed up to keep the dirt and microbes out."

While the microbes were talking the milk was sitting in a sunny spot on the counter and had become quite warm. This made it a great place for the microbes to divide and multiply, which most of them had been very busy doing. The Lactic Acid Microbes were very angry, and hurried about their work of turning the milk sour so that Maggie would not drink it.

After a period of time Maggie came back into the kitchen. "I forgot my chocolate milk. I don't think this milk will taste good," she thought. "I took too many turns on Jennifer's bike. I'll just pour this down the sink."

"Where will we go now?" wondered Micki.

"The milk will be thrown away in the sink, and there is no telling what will happen to us," wailed one of the microbes.

Instead of going down the drain, Micki had a thrilling experience ahead of him.

An Airplane Ride

When Maggie poured the milk into the sink, Micki and some of the other little microbes were left stranded on the rim of the glass in a drop of milk. Even a drop of milk makes a good swimming pool for microbes. Micki just floated around, chuckling at his good fortune in not being poured down the drain as most of the others had been.

He did not have long to gloat over his good luck, soon a big fly lit on the rim of the glass. He looked like a giant to Micki, who was so tiny that the fly could not see him at all.

The fly started to walk around the rim of the glass. He came closer and closer to Micki and the other little microbes. Then he walked right through the drop of milk, and Micki and some of the other microbes caught hold of one of the hairs on the leg of the fly. The fly was not aware of it, but he flew away with them clinging tightly so they would not fall. Micki was surprised to find that there were many other little microbes on the leg of the fly airplane. Many of these microbes Micki had never seen before.

Micki enjoyed the nose dives and the sudden turns as the fly airplane darted up and down, then flew around in a circle. Micki was disappointed when his airplane landed, even though it came to rest on a big piece of bread spread with peanut butter. The peanut butter was moist and rather sticky. Micki and some of his companions were left lying in the soft peanut butter as the fly airplane took off for another flight.

Micki was tired after his exciting ride and dropped off to sleep, buried deep in the soft brown bed. While he was sleeping, he dreamed he was riding through the air on a chocolate airplane. All of a sudden the chocolate plane in his dream crashed into something hard.

Micki awoke with a start and found himself in a mouth filled with bread and peanut butter. The White Teeth Hills were moving up and down, chewing — chewing. Micki crouched down in a crevice in one of the White Hills. He did not want to be chewed up with the bread. There in the crevice of the big White Hill, he found other microbes hiding.

After the bread and peanut butter was all gone, those hungry White Hills bit into a bright red apple. While the White Hills were chewing away on the juicy bites, Micki heard Maggie call,"Mom, I'm going outside again to play with my friends."

It was not long before Micki heard someone say "Hi," Maggie. Give me a bite of your apple."

Maggie stopped, took one more bite and then handed it to her friend, Jennifer.

Of course the microbes were so small that neither of the girls could see them on the spot where Maggie had taken her last bite, but Micki and several little microbes were there just the same. The next instant they were trying to escape being chewed up in Jennifer's mouth as they had in Maggie's only a moment before.

But being chewed up was not half as bad as the next experience Micki encountered.

A New Acquaintance

Jennifer was foolish to take a bite of Maggie's apple. That is such an easy way for microbes to travel from one person to another.

As Micki started down Jennifer's Throat Street toward Tonsil Park, he noticed an odd shaped microbe who seemed to be trying to hide. This new microbe had a long slim body with a little round nob at each end.

Micki had never seen a microbe that looked like this one. He was wondering why this strange little microbe was trying to keep out of sight. Micki tried to be friendly.

"Hello! Why are you trying to hide?"

"Sh!" was the whispered answer. "Don't let anyone know I am here."

"Why not?" asked Micki in a low voice.

"Because some of Jennifer's policemen would try and get rid of me before I have a chance to multiply and divide," murmured the other microbe.

"Who are you? And why would they want to get rid of you?"

"I am Diphtheria Bacillus. I am dangerous! I make people very sick," boasted the strange microbe in a chilling tone.

Micki was frightened and disgusted. "Where did you come from?" he asked.

"I was in Maggie's mouth with you. I traveled to Jennifer's mouth on the apple when you did," replied Diphtheria Bacillus.

"That's funny. I did not see you in Maggie's mouth," remarked Micki.

"That was because I was so busy trying to make Maggie sick. I did my best to give her Diphtheria, but it was no use. I could not make her sick."

"Why couldn't you make her sick?" asked Micki.

"She had been immunized," answered Diphtheria Bacillus.

"What a funny word. What does immunized mean?" questioned Micki.

"Immunized means that the doctor has given Maggie a shot and injected something into her which keeps her from having Diphtheria," complained Diphtheria Bacillus.

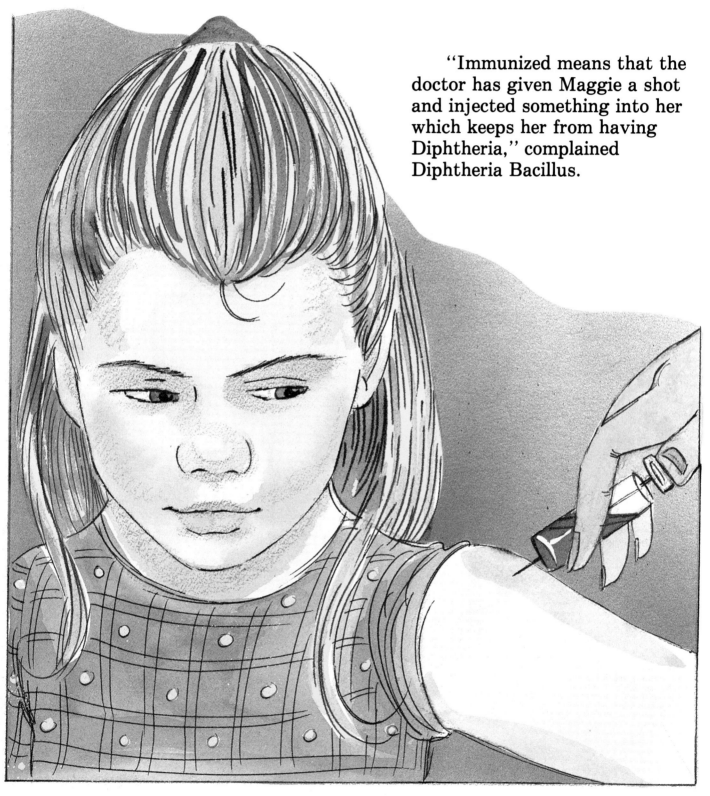

"I have never heard of that before. Is it something new?" asked the surprised Micki.

"No, it is not new. Doctors have been immunizing people for a long time. It makes it very hard for me. I can't divide and multiply."

"Are many people immunized?" asked Micki.

"Nearly all the children are now. If they keep on immunizing everyone, it won't be long until there won't be any of us Diphtheria Microbes at all."

Micki decided he did not like this bad little germ; he was such a wicked fellow. Micki could not help feeling that the world would be a better place without him.

"Why do you like to make people sick?" asked Micki.

"That is all I know how to do. Would you like to come with me and see if I can make Jennifer sick? If she has Immunization Guards we'll try and get out fast," explained the wicked germ.

"No, indeed," answered Micki. "I'm going to get out of Jennifer's Throat Street as fast as I can."

Diphtheria Bacillus laughed a wicked laugh as he carefully looked around to see if there was a place he could hide.

Of course, Jennifer did not know what was happening in her Throat Street and she went happily on, riding her bicycle down the street. Just as she rode around the corner, Brian came running out of his house.

"I'll give you this lemon popsicle if you'll let me ride your bike to the next corner and back," propositioned Brian.

Jennifer decided this was a good idea and made the exchange. However, after only two bites, Jennifer decided she didn't like lemon flavor and would give the popsicle back to Brian. But two bites were more than enough for Micki and many other little microbes to get a firm hold on the cold ice and thus escape from Jennifer's Throat Street.

Out in the warm sunshine on the end of a popsicle was a very bad place for the microbes to be. Not only would the popsicle melt but microbes do not like sunshine. They knew they would probably all die if they had to stay a long time in the hot sun. But they didn't have to worry long because Brian soon returned, riding fast on the bicycle.

"You can have this back, I don't like lemon," said Jennifer as she handed Brian the popsicle.

Brian took the dripping ice and quickly put it into his mouth. Now Micki and many other little microbes found themselves in a new Throat Street, ready for another adventure.

Exploring the White Teeth Hills

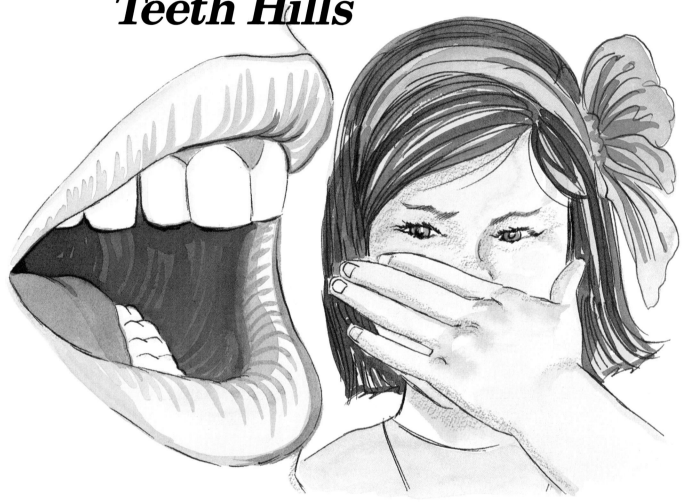

"Well, here we are back in Throat Street again," said Micki to his tiny companions. "Let's see if there is anything different in Brian's White Teeth Hills."

"What is that bad smell?" asked one of the microbes.

"It seems to be coming from the White Hills," replied Micki. After so many visits, Micki felt he knew a great deal about Throat Street.

Micki and all the other little microbes started out to find what was making a bad odor in Brian's White Teeth Hills. All of a sudden they came upon the strangest sight. Deep down in a cavity between two of the big hills, there were hundreds of little microbes swarming all over something brown. They were so busy they did not see Micki and his friends. Micki could not imagine what they were doing.

One of the strange little microbes noticed Micki and his friends and called out, "Come and help us."

Micki moved a little closer, "What are you doing?"

"We are decomposing this food," explained the microbe.

"What does decomposing mean?" asked the inquisitive Micki.

"It means to break it all up, and make the food rot or decay. Brian seldom brushes his teeth, so it is our job to get rid of the food which is left on his teeth," explained the busy microbes.

"What happens to it after you decompose it?" asked Micki.

"Some of it turns into liquid, and some of it turns into gas."

"What makes that bad smell?" questioned Micki.

"The gas from the decomposed food makes the bad odor," explained one microbe.

Just then Micki Microbe noticed a big cavity. "Look at the big cave over there. That would make a good hiding place."

"There are many good hiding places in Brian's White Hills. We are glad he does not clean his teeth, or have the dentist fill up the cavities. If he did, we would have to move to some other Molar Mountains," said one of the microbes. "A long time ago we lived in Jim's White Hills, but we had to move because Jim brushes his teeth every morning and night. Besides a toothbrush, he used that terrible white dental floss. There was never enough food for us to eat."

"He had the dentist fill up every little cavity as soon as it started, so there was no place for us to live," complained another microbe. "Besides that, he ate raw fruits, carrots, celery and apples. They scoured his teeth so clean that there was no place for us to hold on. We did not stay in Jim's Molar Mountains long."

"And he drank so much milk. That made his teeth hard inside, so that it was not easy for us to dig a cave," added another little microbe of the White Hills.

"How do the caves start in the hills?" asked Micki.

"I don't know what causes the first break in the enamel on the outside, but after a tiny hole starts, it gives us a good chance to dig a big hole on the inside. The inside of the hills is softer than the outside, so it is easier to work on," explained one of the microbes.

"I rather like it here, " said Micki. "I think I'll stay a while. Perhaps I could help you decompose some of this food."

"We have good parties in these hills," boasted one of the microbes. "Brian eats lots of soft, sweet food that easily hides in the caves. You won't be sorry if you stay, we have such good times."

So Micki started out to explore Brian's White Teeth Hills with his new friends.

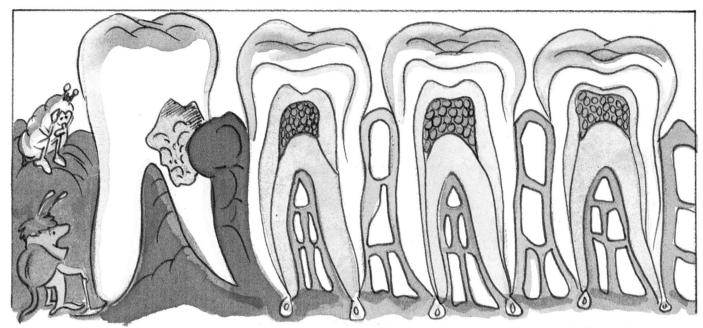

Micki and the little microbes had not gone far in the White Hills when they came upon a new hill that interested Micki. It was a small red hill at the foot of one of the White Hills.

"What is that red hill?" he asked.

"That is Gum Boil Hill," explained one of the little microbes. "You remember we told you that Brian seldom brushes his teeth, and never goes to the dentist to have the holes filled up. Well, when the caves have been there a long time and get very deep, some of the Staphylococcus and Streptococcus Microbes go exploring in the deep cavities. Sometimes they make their way into the very center or nerve of the White Hill. They will divide and multiply until there are so many of them that Brian's White Corpuscle Policmen are called out to fight them. They have a big battle but usually pus is formed and a big red hill appears."

"Does the Gum Boil Hill hurt Brian?" asked Micki.

"Of course it hurts him; wait a minute and you'll see."

Micki and the other little microbes settled down at the foot of the big red hill to see what would happen. In a few minutes Brian put his finger in his mouth. The finger rubbed the red hill which was steadily growing bigger. When Brian took his finger out of his mouth, Micki gasped at what he saw. The bright red hill was swarming with many little microbes which had not been there a moment before.

"Where did they all come from?" gasped Micki.

"That dirty finger left them there," answered a microbe.

"Where could a finger find so many different kinds of microbes?" Micki asked.

"Oh, Brian picks them up everywhere," explained one of the knowledgable microbes. "Some of those microbes came out of his dirty pocket, some came off the money he spent at the store, some were on the handle bars of his bike, a lot of them came off the nose of his dog when he licked Brian's hand. He picks them up everywhere and carries them a long time because he doesn't like to wash his hands."

While the microbes were laughing and talking, Brian thrust his finger into his mouth again to rub the sore gum boil. Of course, Brian did not realize all the little microbes were having such fun, but as he put his finger on the sore spot Micki and many of his new friends were picked up by the finger and carried away.

"My goodness!" exclaimed Micki. "Who would ever imagine that so much dirt and so many microbes could be in one place? There are so many different microbes here I think I'll stay around a while and learn more about them."

But just then Micki heard someone call, "Brian, dinner is ready. Go wash your dirty hands."

And that is how Micki happened on a new adventure.

Micki Visits Impetigo House

Instead of taking time to rub his hands with soap and warm water, Brian turned on the tap, dipped his hands in the running water, and wiped them on the nearest towel. There he left Micki and many other little microbes lying in a moist, dirty spot.

"I don't like it here," cried one of the little microbes. "It is cold and I can't divide when I'm cold."

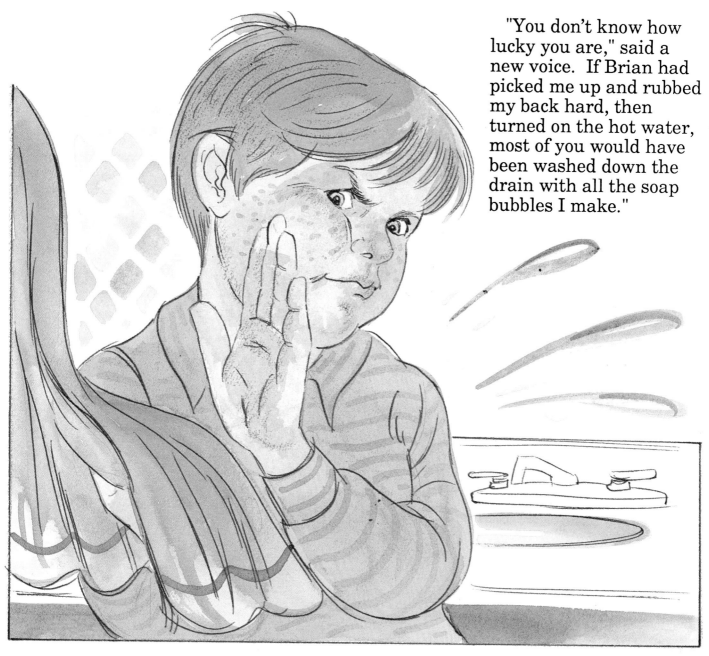

"You don't know how lucky you are," said a new voice. If Brian had picked me up and rubbed my back hard, then turned on the hot water, most of you would have been washed down the drain with all the soap bubbles I make."

"Well, Mr. Towel, you look a sight with all the dirt on you; but look at me, too," complained Wash Basin. "I was spotless and beautiful, now see what Brian has done to my shining face."

"I did my best," wept Faucet, whose tears were dripping down on the basin.

"I think I have the most to complain about," said Tooth Brush. "Brian has not picked me up for weeks. It is terrible to be ignored in such a manner."

While Micki was listening to all the troubles of the bathroom folks, he noticed one of the strange little microbes was very unhappy and decided he would talk to him.

"Why are you so grumpy?" inquired Micki.

"I don't like to be on this towel. I'm an Impetigo Microbe and I can't build a home here. I do hope someone comes soon and takes me away."

As soon as Impetigo had spoken, Tracy came running into the bathroom. Much to the delight of the soap, she vigorously rubbed his back and then rinsed with warm water. When she picked up the towel she wiped her hands right on the spot where all the little microbes lay.

Impetigo was delighted, and he called to the others, "Come with me, and I will show you where I live."

Tracy did not know about the little microbes on her hands, so, when a tiny scratch on her chin started to itch, Tracy rubbed it with the very finger on which Micki and the other little microbes were sitting. It did not take Impetigo long to snuggle down in the little scratch where Tracy had left him.

"Just what I wanted!" squealed Impetigo. "Now watch me divide and multiply." Then he began to swell up like a tiny balloon. He divided and multiplied many, many times.

Micki looked on with amazement. He wondered what these mischievous microbes would do to Tracy's face. "My goodness, Impetigo works fast. Just see how many there are now," exclaimed Micki.

"He has to work fast. He has to build his home while he has a place to build it. Now there are so many of them, soap and water can't wash all of them out," said one of the microbes who had seen Impetigo build his home before.

"What are they doing now?" asked Micki as he saw a little blister forming over the spot where the Impetigo Microbes were working.

"Watch and you'll see," was the answer.

In a few minutes Tracy scratched the tiny blister because it was itching. A drop of water came out of the blister. When it dried it formed a hard roof over the top of Impetigo House.

"That is just what they wanted," laughed a little microbe. "Now their house is built, roof and all. The only way that Impetigo and his family can be disturbed is to put some strong medicine on them that will kill them."

The next morning Tracy carried Micki Microbe and the little Impetigo House to school with her. Of course, she did not know they were there, and it was such a tiny house Mother had not noticed it when she hurried Tracy off to school.

After Tracy put her books away and settled down at her desk, the small scratch started to itch. She scratched the roof off Impetigo House and out popped a tiny drop of water. It looked perfectly clear, but there were hundreds of little microbes floating around in the liquid. Some of it got on Tracy's hand, and some of it spread around on her chin where more little houses were soon built. Micki and some of the little Impetigo Microbes which stayed on Tracy's hand soon found themselves clinging to the side of Tracy's pencil.

Launi, who sat across the aisle, asked to borrow Tracy's pencil. Tracy handed her the pencil, but she did not know that she was handing Launi all those little microbes, too.

It did not take those active little microbes long to find a warm spot on Launi's finger and soon they were settled down in a tiny scratch, getting ready to build another Impetigo House.

It was warm and comfortable on Launi's hand, but Micki was worried. All morning, there in the classroom, Micki could hear several Watch Dogs barking. He wondered what little microbes were trying to get down to Lung House. He thought it might be interesting to find out what all the noise was about.

Another Visit to Windpipe Lane

There was one Old Cough, directly behind Launi, which seemed to bark louder than the rest. Finally, Launi turned around and said to the boy who sat behind her, "Bruce, why don't you cover your mouth when you cough? You sound like you have a cold. You should have stayed home today."

Then Bruce coughed again, and hundreds of tiny particles of moisture came flying out of his mouth. They settled down all over his desk and on Launi's face and hands. Each tiny drop contained hundreds of microbes. Some of them were as big as Micki, but others so small that even Micki could hardly see them. There were some odd looking little microbes that were shaped like little short rods, quite unlike any Micki had ever seen before.

"Well, who are you?" Micki asked.

"We are the Pertussis Bacilli. We live in Windpipe Lane, where we tease Old Cough. We are called the Whooping Cough Germs and we are trying to find a home with someone who has not been immunized."

Just then Launi was thinking about an answer to a difficult arithmetic problem and she put the end of the pencil up to her mouth. This was the chance Impetigo and the Pertussis Bacilli were looking for. Impetigo slipped off to find a tiny scratch on the chin while Micki and the Pertussis found their way into Launi's mouth.

"Come on with us," urged Pertussis. "We're going down to Windpipe Lane to build a home."

"How do you make your home in Windpipe Lane?" asked Micki hesitantly. He wasn't sure he wanted to accompany these microbes.

"We bury ourselves in the soft walls of the Lane, down in the Hairy Forest. Old Cough doesn't like us and tries his best to drive us out. Our biggest problem, however, is that most children have been immunized. We don't get many chances to divide and multiply because too many parents take their children to the doctor for shots, and that means the Corpuscle Policemen will be called out and destroy us.

Micki knew these must be wicked little germs if the policemen wanted to destroy them. "What will you do to Launi if she hasn't been immunized?" he asked.

"We'll multiply in Windpipe Lane for six or seven weeks and give her a terrible cough," boasted one of the Pertussis Bacillus. "In fact, Launi will cough so hard she will almost lose her breath. As she tries to breathe she will make a particular noise which sounds like WHOOP, because of this I'm also known as the Whooping Cough Microbe."

Micki could not understand why some microbes seemed so happy to make children sick. He thought of his old friends, the Pneumo Twins. "Say, if you live in Windpipe Lane, you must know **Pneumo 1 and Pneumo 2**."

"Indeed I do. They are pals of ours. We often try to work together. They'll give the children Pneumonia while we give them Whooping Cough. In fact they might be down in Lung House now if you'd like to go down and visit them. Slide with us over Tongue Hill and continue to the end of Windpipe Lane."

Micki decided this would be a great adventure as well as a chance to say goodbye to this wicked germ. He didn't want to take a chance of being destroyed if the Corpuscle Policemen were called out.

A Visit to Lung House

Micki knew from past experience how to carefully crawl through the Hairy Forest. Each time Old Cough would bark, trying to drive out the Pertussis Bacilli, Micki would crouch very low. The tiny Hairy Forest was moving back and forth rapidly, trying to do its part in getting rid of the microbes. Micki was finally able to make his way to the end of Windpipe Lane where he saw long halls leading into hundreds of little rooms. While he was trying to decide which direction to go, he heard a familiar voice.

"Hey, Micki! Are we glad to see you again! We were just going to have a family party. There are hundreds of us, almost every room is filled; but we're sure we can find space for you."

And that is how Micki met his old pals, the Pneumo Twins and accepted the invitation to a party in Lung House.

The little microbes passed along one of the halls until they came to a small door. When they opened the door, they found that some members of Pneumo's family were having a swimming party.

"Do you always have swimming pools in Lung House?" asked Micki.

"When we have a large family party, we usually have a swimming pool built. You see we are great swimmers," answered Pneumo 1.

"Doesn't that hurt Launi?" asked Micki. He liked Launi and did not want to see her hurt.

"Of course it hurts her. That doesn't make any difference to us, just so we have a good time," laughed several Lof the Pneumococci.

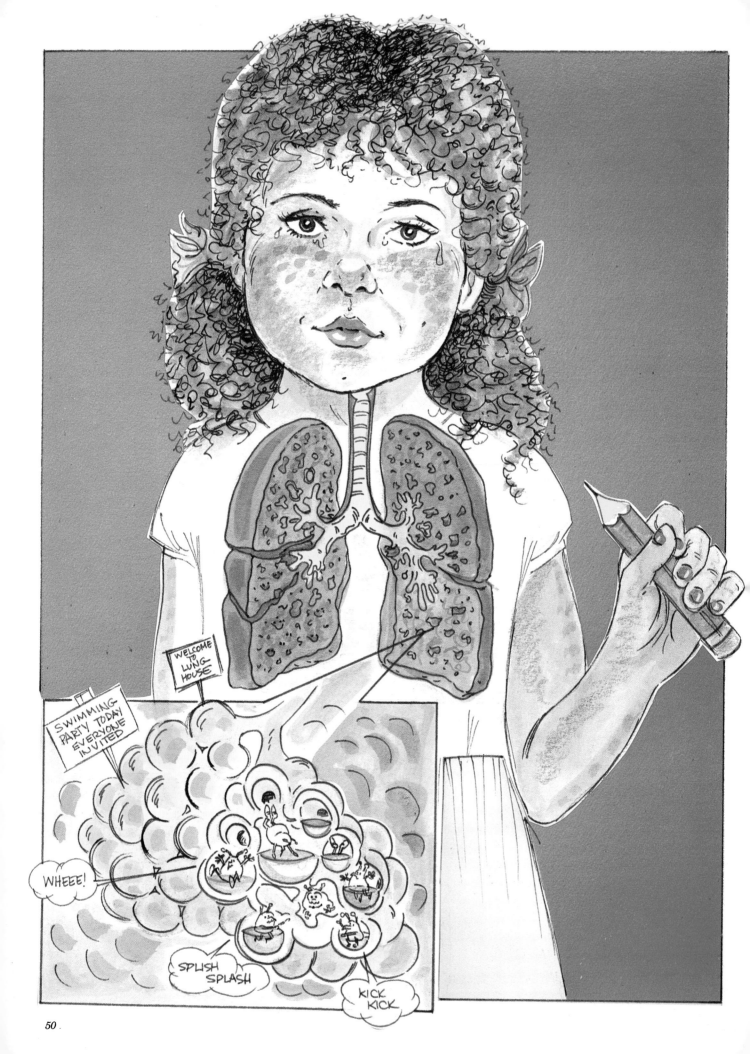

Micki was horrified. He had not realized the Pneumos were such wicked little germs. He decided he must get out of Lung House, away from these terrible microbes. He felt sure something awful was going to happen and he did not want to be around when it occurred.

While Micki was wondering which way to turn to get to the door of Lung House, he saw a huge giant coming down the hall. He was a hundred times bigger than Micki or the Pneumos. Poor little Micki was so frightened he didn't know what to do.

"Pneumo, who is that coming down the hall?" he whispered in a trembling voice.

"Come in here quickly," said the Pneumo Twins, as one of them pulled Micki into a little room. "That is Mr. Leucocyte, one of the White Corpuscle Guards from Blood River. He is trying to catch us. If he finds us, he will call out thousands of policemen and search every room in Lung House for members of our family. The policemen patrol Blood River and when we are having too good a time they come to stop the party and carry us all off to goodness knows where."

"Why do the policemen want to get rid of you and drive you out of your home?" asked Micki.

"Because we are making Launi very sick. The doctor says she has Pneumonia. You see, we don't really belong here. We don't pay any rent, and our family is very rough. We do a lot of damage to Lung House and it takes a long time to clean up after we have had a big party. Our swimming pools have to be dried up and that is quite a job. A doctor will prescribe some medicine to help clean up the mess."

"That White Corpuscle Guard was awfully big and fat. What makes him like that?" asked Micki, still speaking in a whisper.

"The food Launi eats makes him big and fat and strong. She eats lots of vegetables, fruits, whole grain bread, and drinks plenty of milk. Whenever we see the White Corpuscle Guards and policemen big and strong, we know we have very little chance to live," wailed the Pneumo Twins.

Micki put his finger on his head as he started thinking. He seemed to remember having heard something like that before. Then he remembered the little microbes in the White Teeth Hills had said that vegetables, fruits, grains and milk make strong teeth.

"Say, Pneumo," whispered Micki as they crouched there hiding, "the food children eat must be quite important."

"It is important," answered Pneumo 1. "If Launi hadn't eaten all the nourishing food, her Corpuscle Policemen would not be so strong and they could not fight us so hard."

"What chance have we now?" wailed Pneumo 2.

Micki and the Pneumococci stayed in hiding for a long time, hoping the guard would not find them. Finally, the Pneumo Twins decided to creep out into the hall and see what had happened. Everything was still and quiet. They crept out and looked around. Out jumped a fat White Corpuscle Guard. An alarm sounded! Quick as a wink a policeman appeared, grabbed the Pneumococci and started to run.

That was the last Micki saw of the wicked Pneumo Microbes and was he glad!

Micki Learns a Lesson

Micki waited a long time in one of the rooms in Lung House before he had enough courage to look out into the hall again. Cautiously he slid out, hoping he could reach the door without being seen; but when he went round the turn in the hall, there stood a big fat guard. Micki was so frightened that he just stood there unable to move.

"Say, young fellow," said the guard in a loud voice. "What are you doing here? You don't look like one of those bad germs."

Micki could hardly speak, he was shaking so. "I'm Micki Microbe of the Lactic Acid Family. I just came to visit the Pneumo Twins."

"Don't you know better than to play with such bad microbes?" asked the White Corpuscle Guard.

"I didn't know they were bad. They seemed so friendly to me; but I have learned a lesson today," said Micki in a humble voice.

"I hope it has been a lesson to you. Never associate with bad company or you are likely to get into trouble," warned the Corpuscle Guard. "Well, come on Micki. I'll escort you out of Lung House, if you'll try and find your way home to Milky Land.''

"Oh, thank you, Mr. Guard. I'm beginning to get homesick and I would like to see my family again,'' replied Micki.

"You certainly got mixed up with a bad lot of microbes this time,'' said the guard. "Those bad germs started to make Launi sick, but I called out her healthy policemen and we were so strong we were able to defeat the bad microbes.''

While they were talking, the guard led the way to the foot of Windpipe Lane. "So long, Micki!'' he called. "Be a better little microbe from now on.''

Micki was anxious to get out of Windpipe Lane and he climbed the Hairy Forest so fast that Old Watch Dog started barking. It took only one big cough to send Micki flying out into the air.

Launi reached for a kleenex when she felt a tickle in her throat so when Micki came hurtling out, he found himself in the center of the tissue.

Guess who Micki found next to him? His old friend the Impetigo Microbe.

"What are you doing here?" asked Micki in surprise.

"I am so lucky!" answered Impetigo. "I was able to get away on the kleenex when it touched Launi's chin. The rest of my family were destroyed by some ointment Launi's mother put on the cottage we were trying to build. I heard her explain that Tracy's mother telephoned her and told her to watch out for my family. I think all the little Impetigo Houses on Tracy's face were destroyed by the same medicine."

The little microbes were so busy talking they did not notice Launi had put the kleenex down on the table. Cyndee, Launi's little sister, came along and picked it up. "I'm going to help Mother get the kitchen cleaned up so we can make some cookies," and she threw the tissue into the waste basket.

Micki held on tight to Cyndee's warm hand and this was the way he was picked up and carried away to a new and exciting journey.

The Tear Duct Waterfall

Micki had not been on Cyndee's finger very long when he heard her say, "I must have something in my eye."

Cyndee put her finger up to her eye and gently rubbed the corner. Immediately Micki found himself swimming in Salty Lake. It was such a pretty clear lake that Micki decided to float around and find out more about this interesting place. Soon the water changed to a deep blue color and then he seemed to be floating over a deep black hole.

Micki was frightened. "What if I should fall into that deep hole and not be able to get out?"

He looked down through the deep black part of the lake. Suddenly he started to laugh. "I can't sink," he said to himself. "This is deep but there is a thin covering over it."

He knew he could see through it and yet could not fall through. How amazing! If he had known the meaning of the word transparent he might not have thought it so unusual.

Just then he saw something floating past him. It was only an eyelash, but it looked like a huge log to the tiny microbe. As he watched the eyelash move over the surface of the lake, Micki noticed the water was getting deeper and deeper. He swam around the edge trying to find out what was happening. Soon he came to some tiny springs that were pouring salty water into the lake. As the water grew too deep for the rim to hold, it ran over the spillway near Nose Bridge. The bothersome eyelash was washed over the spillway, too, as salty water trickled down Cyndee's cheek.

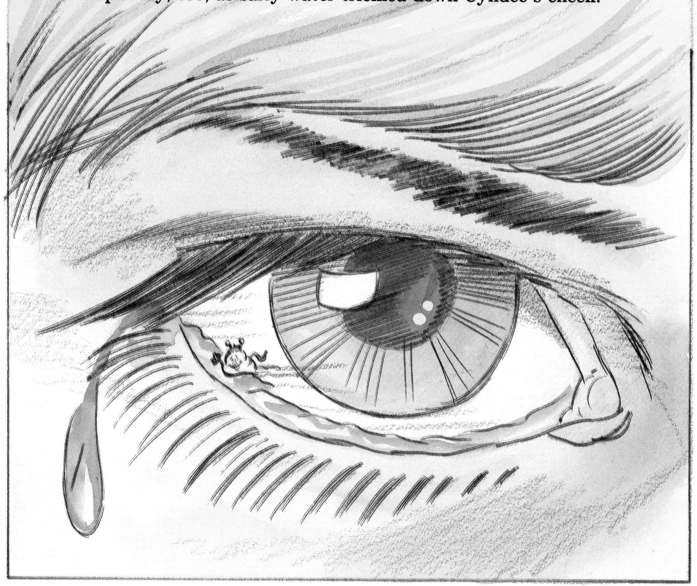

Part of the extra water was being drawn off in the opposite direction. Micki was caught in this swift stream. He was washed over Tear-Duct Waterfall down into a dark passage behind Nose Bridge, into Nose Cave and down to Throat Street.

Micki looked around in amazement. "What do you know about this!" he exclaimed. "Tear-Duct Waterfall empties into Nose Cave and Throat Street. It must be the main highway. All other roads seem to lead into it or out of it."

Micki did not want to go down Throat Street again for fear he would get lost in Lung House so he decided to climb back up and explore Nose Cave.

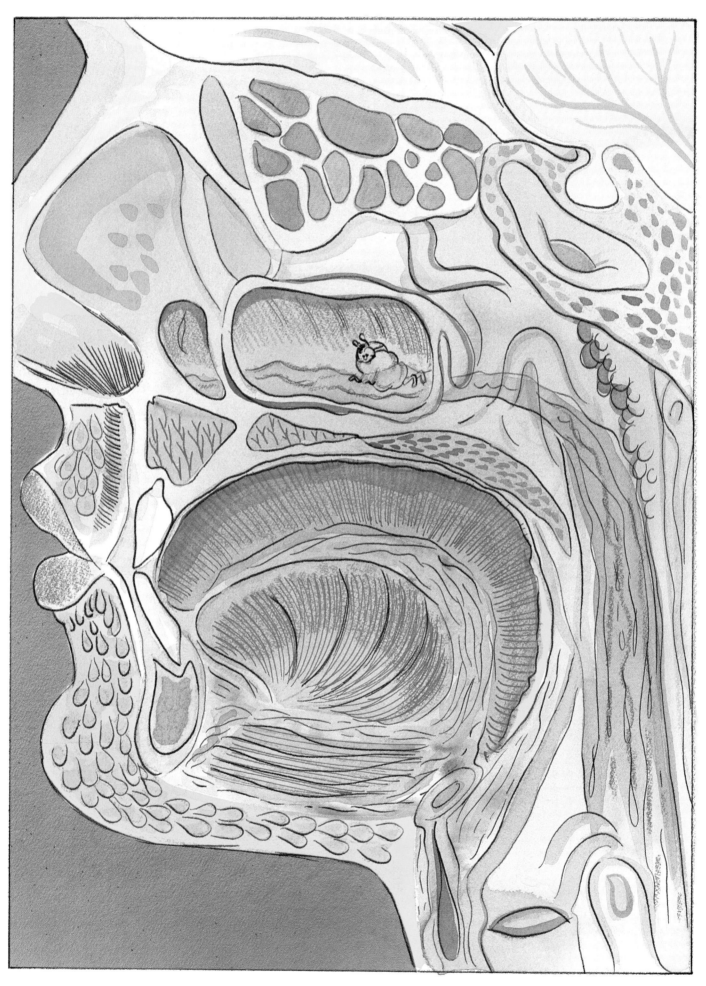

Exploring the Dark Caves

As Micki crept nearer and nearer to the small opening he realized it led into another cave. At first it was so dark he could not see a thing. He thought it was a spooky place.

"Are there any openings to let in some light?" he whispered, hoping there was someone around that might hear him.

"No! There is only one opening to Sinus Cave," spoke a strange little voice not far away.

Micki jumped. "Who are you?" he asked in a startled voice.

"We are the Cold-In-The-Head Virus," sang a little chorus. "We are so small you cannot see us here in the dark, but what a lot of fun we have!"

"What are you doing in Sinus Cave?" asked the inquisitive Micki.

"This is one of our favorite adventure caves, but sometimes it is very dangerous to come in here," replied the little chorus.

"Why is it dangerous?" whispered Micki.

"Because there is only one opening into the cave. If that gets closed, we can't get out."

"What do you do then?" asked Micki.

"Oh, we just kick up such a fuss the doctor has to open the passage and release us."

Micki decided these wicked virus would not be good companions and he had better get through the tiny opening he had found. He left Sinus Cave and continued his journey to the top of Nose Hill. Here he saw more of the Cold-In-The-Head Virus busily at work making streams of water flow out of Cyndee's Nose Cave.

"How tiny they are!" exclaimed Micki in amazement.

"Yes, we are called Virus because we can't be seen, even in the microscope," explained some of the tiny virus that had seen Micki's surprise. "We are so small that we can get away with a lot of mischief. We are often blamed for things we don't do, but we can cause a lot of trouble, too."

By this time Micki had reached the top of the hill which leads from Nose Cave down into Throat Street. He decided he should slide down the hill on a droplet of moisture and get away from the Cold-In-The-Head Virus before Cyndee's policemen were called in to fight them.

"Whee!" squealed Micki as he sped down the steep hill toward Mouth Valley. Before he reached the bottom of the hill he struck something soft and spongy which held him fast. While he was trying to figure out what happened, he saw some long chains of microbes playing crack the whip.

Micki tried to stand up on the spongy surface. "I remember who you are," he said to the chain-like microbes. "You are the wicked Streptococci. What are you doing here? Where am I?"

ZOOOP!

"Oh! You just landed on Adenoid Prairie," replied the playful microbes. "It's a big microbe playground between Nose Cave and Throat Street. Stay with us and have some fun!"

Micki knew he did not want to get mixed up again with these wicked Streps. While he was considering the best way to get away from this microbe playground, Cyndee blew her nose very hard. There was a loud noise which seemed to come from Nose Cave. The little microbes were picked up by a strong suction and drawn into a dark narrow passage.

"Where are we?" Micki asked one of the Streptococci.

"This is the Eustachian (u-sta-ke-an) Tube. It leads to Middle Ear Cave — where we'll have some fun!" squealed the excited little microbes.

The chains of microbes pushed and crowded until they finally were in Middle Ear Cave. There they found they could go no farther. A thin, pearly white wall shut off all chance of escape through Ear Canal to the outside world.

"That wall won't be hard to break through," boasted one microbe.

"It may look thin and delicate, but that is Ear Drum and it will take us a long time to break through it and get out of here," explained some of the others.

"We will have to divide and multiply very fast so there will be more of us to break down the wall," some of the Streps cried.

All of the Streptococci began to swell up like tiny balloons. Then they grew smaller and smaller in the middle until each one divided into two microbes. The chains grew longer and longer until some of them broke away and started new chains.

Micki crept cautiously away from the bad microbes. He wanted to find some way out of Middle Ear Cave. He tried to go back through the Eustachian Tube but found the passage blocked with the wicked germs and White Corpuscle Policemen fighting a fierce battle.

Suddenly Micki noticed a tiny opening in the wall at the back of Ear Cave. "If I reach that opening maybe I can get out of here before a policeman comes after me."

As Micki worked himself toward the mysterious opening at the back of Ear Cave, he saw a few of the long chains of Streptococci slip quietly through the small opening and disappear.

"That must be one way out," thought Micki as he followed them.

When he reached the little doorway, he looked back and saw the pearly white Ear Drum beginning to turn pink.

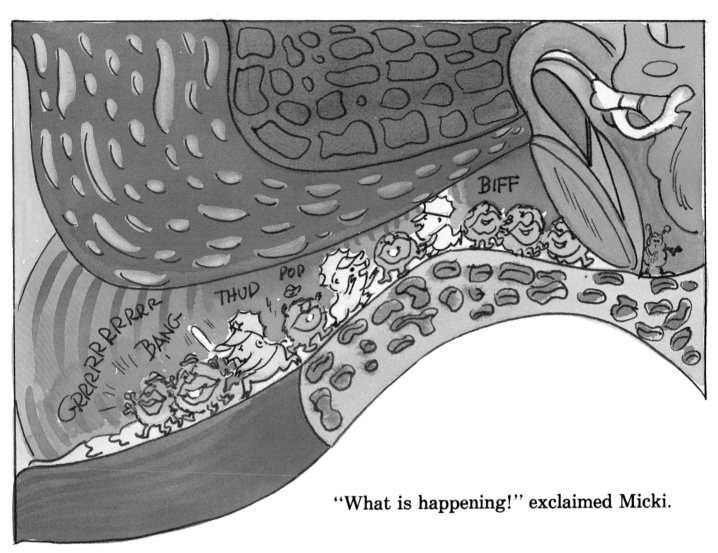

"What is happening!" exclaimed Micki.

He stood there watching the Streps dividing and multiplying as fast as they could, pushing harder and harder against Ear Drum. By this time, Ear Cave was swarming with brave Corpuscle Policemen and wicked microbes fighting a real battle. As policemen and microbes were overcome, they fell in a heap forming a steadily growing mass of pus.

"I must find a way out of here," thought Micki. He crept along a narrow passageway until he came to an opening filled with hundreds of tiny caves. He wandered through many little caves, but always came back to the place where he had first entered Mastoid Cave. Then, seeing one of the chains of Streptococci, Micki asked, "Is there another way out of this cave?"

"There is only one way in or out of Mastoid Cave, and that is the tunnel which leads back to Ear Cave," replied one of the Streps.

"What are all you Streps doing in Mastoid Cave?" asked the inquisitive Micki.

"We are doing the same thing the Streps are doing in Ear Cave. We multiply until the Corpuscle Policemen come and then we have a good fight. These little caves fill up with pus as a result of the battle. There is no way for the pus to get out, so it piles up until it causes a very bad pain," explained a *Streptococcus* gruffly.

"How terrible! You should be ashamed!" remarked the shocked Micki.

"Why? You can't blame us. Cyndee blew her nose too hard and drove us into the Eustachian Tube. There was no place for us to go, except Middle Ear Cave. You saw how crowded it was in the first cave, so we came in here," replied one of the Streps.

"This is a bad place for me to be. I must get back to Ear Cave. At least there is a chance I can get out of there," thought Micki.

As he crept along the narrow tunnel back to Ear Cave he heard a peculiar loud noise. Suddenly he realized it was Cyndee crying. "Those wicked microbes!" exclaimed Micki. "They have caused Cyndee so much pain, they are making her cry."

When he reached the opening into Ear Cave, he was surprised at what had happened during his absence.

Ear Drum was fiery red and bulging way out. He watched the thin, red wall gradually growing thinner and weaker in one spot, until finally it broke in a jagged hole. What excitement there was then! The chains of little microbes began to scramble and push to get out of Ear Cave.

Suddenly Micki realized Cyndee had stopped crying. He heard her say, "Mother, my ear doesn't hurt now, but something is running out of it."

"Cyndee, you must have an ear infection," said Mother. "Now that the pus is escaping, your ear should feel better, but if it still hurts in the morning I'll call Dr. James."

A bad pain in the left ear caused Cyndee to wake up several times in the night, so first thing in the morning Mother called Dr. James and explained the ear problem.

Of course the doctor did not want Cyndee to have all that pain so she told Mother to come immediately to her office.

When Mother and Cyndee arrived, Dr. James took an instrument which had a tiny light in the end of it and looked in both of Cyndee's ears.

Micki heard the doctor say, "The right ear is draining, but I will have to put a tiny tube in the left ear drum to let the pus out. The drum is very red and bulging. The microbes get into the middle ear and if they do not escape soon enough, they back up into the little channel which leads from the middle ear to the mastoid. So you see a bad earache is a warning signal to call me and get some medicine to help kill those bad microbes."

Micki was concerned about whether or not it would hurt Cyndee when the tube was put into the ear. He heard Dr. James explain to Cyndee that she would be sound asleep and would not feel any pain.

Dr. James was so careful it did not hurt Cyndee, and now that all the microbes could escape, the pain would soon be gone.

After Mother stopped at the pharmacist for some medicine she took Cyndee home and told her to rest awhile on her bed. She put a clean towel over the pillow and Cyndee was soon asleep.

While all this was happening, Micki had cautiously crept through the jagged hole in the right ear drum. When he passed through the little opening he could see light at the far end of the passage down Ear Canal. As he journeyed down the canal, he passed orange colored wax along the banks. He laughed as he saw some wicked germs trying to get out of the wax which held them fast and would not let them go. From all his adventures he had learned a great deal. He knew Ear Drum was very sensitive, and anything that touched it made it pain terribly; so wax was there to protect the outside of Ear Drum from any intruders such as germs, insects and dirt.

It took Micki a long time to make his journey down Ear Canal. As he arrived near the opening, he found himself falling out of the ear into a towel spread over the pillow. All about him were chains of Streptococci which had also come out of Middle Ear Cave. He could not believe so many microbes could be in one place.

Micki rested on the warm towel wondering what new and exciting place he could visit now.

Micki Meets a Strange Hitch Hiker

Micki Microbe had rested on the towel only a short time when he heard Mother call Launi. "Please bring me a clean towel, and throw this dirty one in the clothes hamper on your way out."

Micki had no idea where Launi was going, but he decided it would be more fun to get a ride on Launi's warm hand than join the dirty clothes in the hamper. He held on tight and hid between her fingers when she ran outside to play. Micki knew the bright sunshine was not good for microbes and if he stayed out in it too long he could be destroyed.

Launi was soon joined by some of her friends and they hurried down the street and entered a large building for a gymnastics class. Almost immediately Launi performed a handspring and Micki found himself left on the edge of a large blue mat.

As Micki looked around at his new surroundings, he noticed a strange little fellow lying on the mat beside him. Micki wondered if he really was a microbe. He looked something like one, but there was a difference which puzzled Micki.

"Are you hitch-hiking, too?" the stranger suddenly asked.

"I'm out adventuring, but I guess you could call it hitch-hiking. My name is Micki Microbe. What is your name? I don't think we have met before."

"Glad to know you! I am Tricho Phyton," (tri-ko-fit-on) replied the stranger. "I belong to the Fungus Family."

"Where do you live? What do you do?" asked the curious Micki.

"I live where there is moisture. Some members of my family live on moist fruits and vegetables which have been standing for a long time. We can live almost any place where there is moisture. I like especially to live in the Sweat Gland Tunnels deep down in the flesh of the feet between the toes," replied Tricho Phyton.

"What a peculiar place to live! Do you cause disease like some of the microbes do?" asked Micki.

"Well, I suppose you would call it a disease. It is usually called Athlete's Foot. It's a silly nick-name, if you want my opinion," replied Tricho Phyton.

"Where did you get that name?" asked Micki.

"It is called Athlete's Foot because so many athletes have it. They pick us up in gymnasiums, around swimming pools, in showers, in locker rooms and almost any place where floors are generally damp."

"You said you are hitch-hiking. Where are you going?" asked Micki.

"I am waiting for a bare foot to pick me up," replied Tricho Phyton. "I just left a foot where I have been living for some time. I wanted to make me a new home because there were so many of my family in our old home."

Just then Kent stepped out to do a handspring and pressed his damp foot down on the two adventurers sitting on the mat. Kent could not feel them of course because they were so tiny.

"Hurrah! We're off! Come with me and I'll show you my house," cried Tricho Phyton.

After a journey across the bottom of Kent's foot, Micki saw where Tricho Phyton planned to build his home between two toes.

"First I will build a little water blister roof over my house," explained Tricho Phyton. "We have a hard time keeping the roofs on our houses because they are always being scratched or rubbed off. It doesn't matter though because we grow fast and soon there are so many of us it doesn't take long to build a new roof; then when living conditions are not the way we like them, we turn into spores and go to sleep."

"What is a spore?" asked Micki.

"When we turn into spores, we form a protective coat around ourselves and sometimes sleep many months that way. When living conditions are good again, we wake up and go on working as we did before," explained Tricho Phyton.

The microbes lived on Kent's foot for some time and Micki enjoyed watching the Tricho Phytons grow and start building a tract of homes.

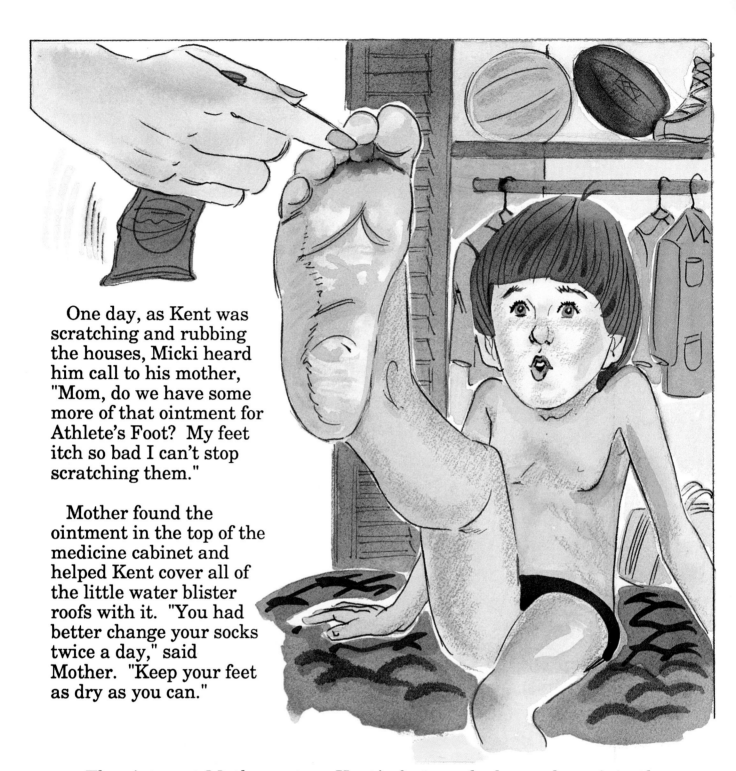

One day, as Kent was scratching and rubbing the houses, Micki heard him call to his mother, "Mom, do we have some more of that ointment for Athlete's Foot? My feet itch so bad I can't stop scratching them."

Mother found the ointment in the top of the medicine cabinet and helped Kent cover all of the little water blister roofs with it. "You had better change your socks twice a day," said Mother. "Keep your feet as dry as you can."

The ointment Mother put on Kent's feet reached way down into the Sweat Gland Tunnels and made it most uncomfortable for Tricho Phyton and his family.

"Micki," Tricho said, "you would be wise to leave here if you can. This medicine is making me so weak I can't travel, so I think I'll turn into a spore and go to sleep. Perhaps in a few weeks I'll wake up and meet you again in our travels."

Lacty Meets
Mr. Phagocyte

For several days Micki hitch-hiked about on fingers, handkerchiefs, glasses, apples, toys, candy wrappers, money and other things. He even had another thrilling ride on a fly airplane. Then all of a sudden he found himself deposited on the rim of a glass, and much to his delight he found himself surrounded by other members of his family. He was back home in that familiar white liquid—milk.

How Micki enjoyed himself, telling his family about his adventures! They were surprised at all the strange places he had visited and all the different kinds of microbes he had met.

Micki's little brother, Lacty, would not stop asking questions. Like Micki, he was very curious. Finally he asked Micki to take him along on his next hitch-hiking trip. Micki wasn't sure he wanted to leave home so soon again; but Lacty was so anxious to go that Micki told him to stay close by, and when someone picked up the glass, to hold tight to the warm moist hand.

They did not have to wait long until Rodney picked up the glass and the two tiny microbes attached themselves to his thumb.

Micki told Lacty to hold on tight because he knew from experience they would meet many new microbes. "Most of these microbes around us are not harmful," he explained, "but we'll have to watch out for the wicked germs."

Lacty was surprised at all the activity around him; but he was even more startled when he heard a loud "Ouch!"

Rodney had gone into the garage to pick up a piece of wood. He had run a sharp sliver into his finger close to the nail where the little microbes lay.

A bright red drop of blood immediately came to the surface.

"Micki, what is that?" cried Lacty in alarm.

"Don't get excited, Lacty. It is only blood from Blood River. See, there is Mr. Phagocyte of the White Corpuscle Police Force. He has been called out by Mr. T, one of Rodney's guards, to be ready for action. He doesn't seem to be busy, so perhaps you can get acquainted with him."

Edging over closer to the red drop, Micki spoke to Mr. Phagocyte. "I have met many White Corpuscle Policemen before, but I want my little brother, Lacty, to meet you. I want him to see how hard you policemen work to get rid of bad microbes."

"You little fellows must watch your step, because there may be a problem here," said the friendly policeman.

"What happened a few minutes ago to make that blood come out of Blood River?" asked Lacty.

"Rodney's finger picked up a sliver. That may mean trouble, so I have been called out to patrol the neighborhood."

"Are there bad germs around?" asked Micki.

"Fingers are always picking up microbes, and an open cut or scratch like this permits them to get inside. A break in the skin is always a danger point. I am cruising around to watch for any intruders. Try to keep out of mischief," advised Mr. Phagocyte.

"I like him, Micki. He seems so jolly and kind," said Lacty.

"He is a good friend if you don't get into mischief and become too friendly with the bad microbes," replied Micki. "Ho, hum!" he yawned. "I'm sleepy. Nothing much seems to be happening, so let's snuggle down here and take a nap while everything is quiet."

After a while Micki sat up and looked around. There was a large white spot under the skin where the sliver had pierced the finger.

Micki nudged Lacty. "Wake up, little fellow, things are beginning to happen!"

Lacty stretched and yawned. "What's the matter?" he asked.

"See that white spot around the sliver? That means White Corpuscle Policemen are fighting bad microbes there," explained Micki.

While they were talking, they saw something bright and shiny coming closer and closer to the spot where the policemen were working so hard.

"What is it Micki?" asked Lacty in an excited voice.

"It's a needle! Rodney must be going to open the sore spot to let the pus out," answered Micki. "If you want to see some excitement, Lacty, watch closely. See those little microbes clinging to the end of the needle? That means Rodney didn't sterilize the needle before he started to use it."

When the needle plunged into the white spot, a drop of yellow pus oozed out. The White Corpuscle Policemen poked his head out and said, "What did I tell you, Micki? I knew there would be trouble here. Now, to make things worse, Rodney has just put more bad microbes in here."

"What are you going to do, Mr. Phagocyte?" asked Micki.

"We will do all we can to fight the infection, but it will be a hard job. You had better get away from this place because I think we are going to need some help from some kind of disinfectant; that will mean the end of all microbes around here."

"Let us know what happens, Mr. Phagocyte," called Micki as he led Lacty away from the battle scene.

The two little microbes found a safe hiding place far down between the fingers. They had to crouch down low and hold tight each time Rodney washed his hands because they wanted to stay around and talk to Mr. Phagocyte again.

After a couple of days they were tired of sitting around and were trying to decide where to look for another adventure when Mr. Phagocyte came and sat down beside them.

"I'm all tired out, but it looks as if the job is about over," he said wearily. "Why wasn't Rodney more careful? You would think he would know enough to sterilize a needle before sticking it in a sore spot and try to remove a sliver. I'm always hearing about the careless things people do. They take a chance of starting a serious infection, and expect us policemen to protect them."

Micki and Lacty were happy to hear that with the assistance of the medicine the White Corpuscle Policemen were able to overcome the bad microbes. They decided to tell the tired policeman goodbye so he could get some rest before he was called to another battle.

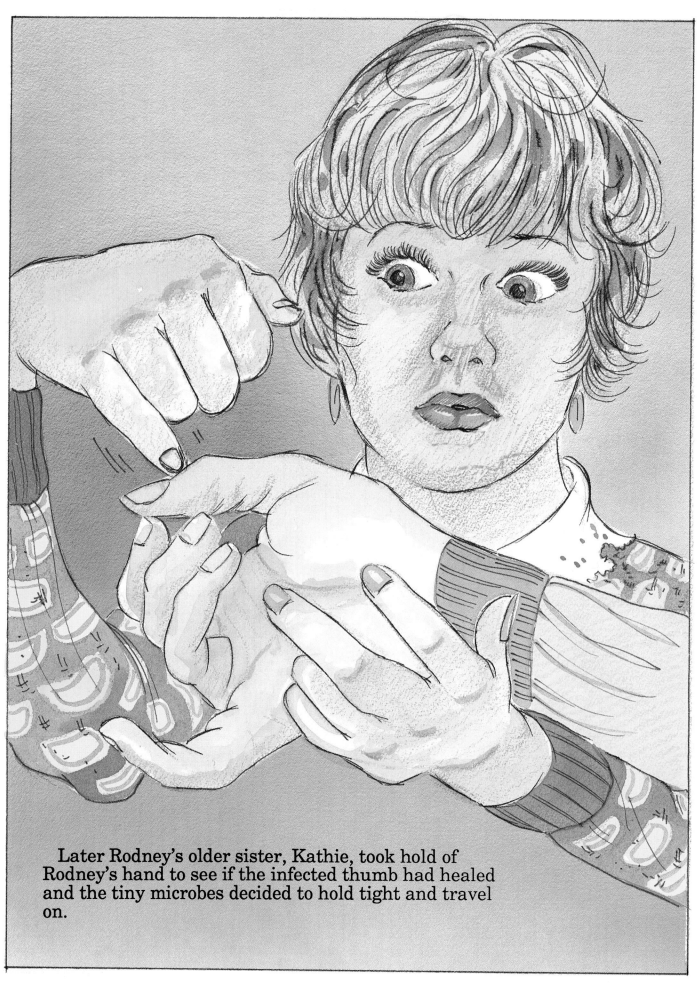

Later Rodney's older sister, Kathie, took hold of Rodney's hand to see if the infected thumb had healed and the tiny microbes decided to hold tight and travel on.

The Rip Van Winkle Microbe

Micki and Lacty had just found a nice resting spot on Kathie's hand when she ran out the door calling, "Bye Mom! Bye Dad! I'm off to my babysitting job at the Derricks. I have to get dinner for all those kids."

When Kathie arrived, Mrs. Derrick told her dinner was ready in the oven, but to heat the string beans which were in a bottle in the cupboard. "Aunt Trish has taken to home gardening and she has sent over a jar of her home canned beans," she explained.

As Kathie opened the beans Micki and Lacty dropped into the liquid. "We certainly thumbed a good ride this time," chuckled Micki. "Fingers carry us to the most unexpected places. Look at that strange object over there."

"What is it Micki? Is it a microbe?" asked Lacty.

"I don't know. I have never seen anything like it before. It is still and quiet, as if it were dead," whispered Micki.

As they watched and wondered, a rod-shaped microbe came floating by. Micki knew it was a member of the Bacillus Family because of its shape. Micki called to the Bacillus and asked what the queer shriveled-up object was.

"That's old Rip Van Winkle!" laughed the Bacillus.

"Rip Van Winkle!" said Micki with a puzzled look. "And who are you?"

"I am Botulinus Bacillus, and Rip Van Winkle is a brother of mine. He didn't wake up when the rest of us did and he will have to sleep for a long time now. That is why we call him Rip Van Winkle."

"Why will he have to sleep for such a long time?"

"Because he can't wake up while these beans are open to the air. You see, he is a Botulinus Spore and can only wake up when there is no air present."

"Why do you turn into spores?" asked Lacty.

"We turn into spores to protect ourselves from heat or lack of moisture. We shrink until we are oval and small, and form a shell-like coat around ourselves," explained Botulinus Bacillus. "When these beans were cooked, they were not heated enough to kill us. The heat was most uncomfortable, so we turned into spores. We were harmless then, but as soon as the bottle was sealed tight so no air could get in, it was possible for us to wake up and make our Botulinus Poison."

"How did you get into the beans in the first place?" asked Micki.

"We were in the soil when the beans were in the garden. If the beans had been eaten raw, or cooked but not sealed in a bottle, we could have done no harm."

"Why not?" asked Lacty.

"Because, as I said, we can only make our poison when food is sealed tight in a can or bottle with no air present," explained Botulinus Bacillus.

"Do you make Botulinus Poison in all home canned foods?" asked Micki.

"Oh, no! Only once in a while we get into vegetables while they are in the garden, and then there are only a few vegetables in which we can grow. We can make Botulinus Poison only in non-acid vegetables such as peas, string beans, carrots and beets. We can make the poison only when food has not been cooked enough to kill all of the spores," replied Botulinus Bacillus.

"Do you live in the canned foods we buy at the store?" asked Micki.

"Oh, no, hardly ever," he answered regretfully. "Food companies have learned how to can food safely by cooking it long enough and with enough heat to make sure all the Botulinus Spores are destroyed. We spores can stand only so much heat."

"Can't people tell when you have made the poison in the food?" Lacty wanted to know.

"No! Generally there is no odor to the poison and the food appears good. If a can is bulging or leaking it may be a sign we are multiplying inside the can. Even one drop of the liquid is enough to make a person very ill," boasted Botulinus Bacillus.

"How terrible!" shuddered Micki.

Botulinus Bacillus looked about carefully to see if anyone were listening. Then he swam close to Micki and Lacty. "I'll tell you a secret, if you won't tell anyone," whispered the wicked microbe. "If the poisoned food is boiled for thirty minutes all the poison will be destroyed."

"Do you mean that simply boiling the poisoned food for thirty minutes will make the food safe to eat?" asked Micki in amazement.

"Yes," whispered the Bacillus. "It doesn't always take even that long, but sometimes some of us are hidden in the middle of a bean where it takes longer for heat to reach us."

Micki sat there wondering if there were any way he could warn Kathie about the poison in the beans.

While he was thinking, he felt a sudden jolting and shaking of the bottle. He clutched little Lacty and grabbed the rim. Then Micki laughed with relief as he realized Kathie had poured the beans into a pan and placed it on the stove.

"Oh, Lacty, I am so glad! Kathie is going to heat those beans. Now if she will only boil them for half an hour," cried Micki.

The two little microbes could see the clock on the shelf as it ticked off the minutes. "We will note the time the beans begin to boil and see if they boil long enough," whispered Micki.

So he and Lacty looked down from their safe seat on the bottle rim and carefully counted the minutes.

"One . . . two . . . three . . . four . . ."

All went well for ten minutes; then Kathie came to the stove to take the beans off.

Micki and Lacty were so excited they almost fell off the bottle. But they could not shout loudly enough to make anyone hear.

Just as Kathie reached for the pan, the telephone rang. She put the pan down and the beans went on bubbling and boiling.

"Micki, I'm certainly glad that phone rang," exclaimed Lacty.

But Micki was busy counting the minutes as they ticked on.

"Eleven . . . twelve . . . thirteen . . . fourteen . . . fifteen." Half of the thirty minutes had passed and Kathie was still talking to her friend, Jenny, about a homework assignment in science for the next day.

"Seventeen . . . eighteen . . . nineteen . . . twenty," Micki continued to count.

Just as he counted to twenty-one he heard Kathie say, "Gotta go! Dinner's ready for the kids." She walked over to the stove, but before she had time to pick up the pan of beans, Baby Dan started to cry. He had pinched his finger in the door and let out a terrible scream.

Kathie ran over to pick up Danny and comfort him while Micki continued to count. "...twenty-seven...twenty-eight...twenty-nine...thirty!" he shouted. "Now Kathie can take the beans off, for all the poison has been destroyed! The family can eat them in safety."

Micki and Lacty sat there on the rim of the bottle, shaking with relief and excitement. "Are you through adventuring?" asked Micki.

"I think I have had enough hitch-hiking for a while," replied Lacty. "I would like to go back home and tell our family about all the exciting adventures we have had."

"I don't think we will have to wait long," said Micki encouragingly. "Look at all the milk on the table. Someone is sure to come along and pick us up. We should be able to hitch a ride to one of those glasses."

And that is exactly what happened. The last we know, Micki and Lacty were telling all their family members about their exciting experiences. Where they went from there, no one seems to know; however, at some late date they probably took off to see what new adventures they could find.